A Garden of Whales

by Maggie Steincrohn Davis
Illustrated by Jennifer Barrett O'Connell

FIREFLY BOOKS

A FIREFLY BOOK

Published by Firefly Books Ltd.
First published by Camden House Publishing
Text copyright © 1993 by Maggie Steincrohn Davis
Illustrations copyright © 1993 by Jennifer Barrett O'Connell

Fourth Printing, 2002

Library of Congress Cataloging-in-Publication Data

Davis, Maggie S., 1942– A garden of whales / written by Maggie Steincrohn Davis ; illustrated by Jennifer Barrett O'Connell. – 1st ed.
p.   cm. ISBN 0-944475-36-1 : $16.95. ISBN 0-944475-35-3 (pbk.): $6.95 J. O'Connell, Jennifer Barrett, ill. II. Title. PZ7.D2952Gar 1993 [E] --dc20 92-34411 CIP AC

Published in Canada by
Firefly Books Ltd.
3680 Victoria Park Avenue
Willowdale, Ontario
Canada M2H 3K1

Published in the United States by
Firefly Books (U.S.) Inc.
P.O. Box 1338, Ellicott Station
Buffalo, New York 14205

"Magic Words"from *Eskimo Songs and Stories*.
Selected and translated by Edward Field.
(Delacourt Press/Seymour Lawrence. 1973.)

Design by Elizabeth Nelson
Printed by Tien Wah Press, Singapore

The Publisher acknowledges the financial support of the Government of Canada through the Book Publishing Industry Development Program for our publishing activities.

For the whales—they have so much to teach us
M.S.D.

For Kevin—with love and many thanks
J.B.O.

MAGIC WORDS

In the very earliest time,
when both people and animals lived on earth,
a person could become an animal if he wanted to
and an animal could become a human being.
Sometimes they were people
and sometimes animals
and there was no difference.
All spoke the same language.
That was the time when words were like magic.
The human mind had mysterious powers.
A word spoken by chance
might have strange consequences.
It would suddenly come alive
and what people wanted to happen could happen—
all you had to do was say it.
Nobody can explain this:
That's the way it was.

from *Eskimo Songs and Stories*

Last night in my tub, in my tub while I scrubbed, I dreamed that I lived in the sea with the Whales.

Magnificent Whales. Mysterious Whales. Mystical, Musical, Mountainous Whales.

I heard their flukes slapping. I saw their skins shimmering. The Whales were singing their heartsongs.

They sang how Whales came to live in the sea, that children once rode upon Whales in the sea—natives give thanks for the Whales in the sea.

In the sea, in the sea, the Whales sang to me. They breathed and their breath was the breath of the sea.

Then deep in my dream, I trembled. I dreamed that danger surrounded the Whales. I dreamed it surrounded the innocent Whales.

"Whales!" I cried. "Whales! Swim away!"

Wheeling around them with rose-colored light, spinning around them in circles of light, circling the Whales in rings of rose light, I raced to comfort the Whales. I tried to rescue the Whales.

But nothing I did helped the Whales.

Awash in my tub, I thought up a plan. I thought up a plan to bring back the Whales. I roused all my friends to help the Great Whales. From all the world over came help for the Whales.

"Whales!" we cried. "Give us your tears. Your tears are the seeds we will plant in a garden. Each will take root in our secret whale garden. Seeds that we plant will be tears of the Whales!"

Up from the sea rose the Ghosts of the Whales. Up from the gray, empty sea rose the Whales—Blue Whales and Humpbacks, Gray Whales and Fins—they rained down their tears on our secret whale garden.

Families of Whales were reborn in our garden. They grew and they bloomed in our garden of Whales.

In the dark of the night, when the time was just right, when the time was just right, we took up the Whales. We took up the Whales in the dark of the night, and slipped them into the sea from our garden. The Whales all rejoiced that had bloomed in our garden.

Nations of Whales. Celebrations of Whales.
The whole Earth resounded with sounds of the Whales.

I wish that I were a Whale tonight. I wish that I were a Whale of a Whale.

A clever old Whale, sharing my secrets. A kindly old Whale, loving my own. A kingly old Whale ruling safe waters.

I am a Whale. The sea is my home. The welcoming, bloom-again sea is my home.

Ken Woisard

Kevin O'Connell

Maggie Steincrohn Davis lives in Blue Hill, Maine and is the author of several books for young people. She is a flower essence practitioner, lay homeopath and herbalist. Maggie says about *A Garden of Whales*: "I wish we could bring back whales to the sea by growing them in gardens, but we can't. We must, while they are still with us, honor whales' right to exist. We must honor all beings who rely on us, by using only our fair share of earth's gifts. This we must do through service—through action—and not just with our eager pounding hearts."

Jennifer Barrett O'Connell spent many childhood hours in her room drawing on spiral pads and traveling to the magical worlds of her imagination that inspire her work today. A graduate of the Philadelphia College of Art, she has been a freelance illustrator and designer since 1982. She is the illustrator of three children's books, including the Christopher Award winners *Promise Not To Tell* and *Imagine That!*. Jennifer lives in Bethesda, Maryland with her husband Kevin and children Bethany and Brendan.